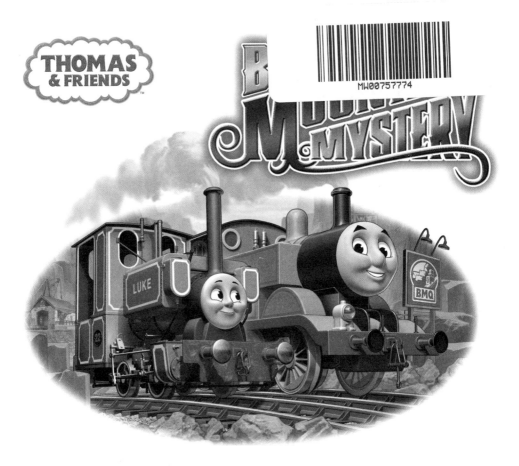

Illustrated by Tommy Stubbs

A GOLDEN BOOK • NEW YORK

CREATED BY BRITT ALLCROFT
Thomas the Tank Engine & Friends™

Based on The Railway Series by The Reverend W Awdry.
© 2012 Gullane (Thomas) LLC.
Thomas the Tank Engine & Friends and Thomas & Friends are trademarks of Gullane (Thomas) Limited.
HIT and the HIT Entertainment logo are trademarks of HIT Entertainment Limited.
All rights reserved. Published in the United States by Golden Books, an imprint of Random House Children's Books,
a division of Random House, Inc., 1745 Broadway, New York, NY 10019, and in Canada by Random House of Canada
Limited, Toronto. Golden Books, A Golden Book, A Little Golden Book, the G colophon, and the distinctive gold spine
are registered trademarks of Random House, Inc.
randomhouse.com/kids
www.thomasandfriends.com
ISBN: 978-0-307-97590-4
Printed in the United States of America
10 9 8 7 6
Random House Children's Books supports the First Amendment and celebrates the right to read.

It was a busy day at the Blue Mountain Quarry. Rusty shunted trucks of slate. Owen lifted equipment up and down the rocky walls.

The Narrow Gauge quarry engines were smaller and lighter than the other engines. They had special tracks.

Paxton, a visiting Diesel, was impressed by how hard they all worked.

Suddenly, there was a loud noise. Giant stones were falling from Blondin Bridge! Rheneas tried to stop, but his heavy trucks pushed him toward the bridge.

Rheneas rolled
across the bridge
just in time!

Unfortunately, Paxton
was buried under
some fallen stones.
He was all right,
but he needed
repairs.

Thomas went to the quarry to work in Paxton's place. "I like working with my Narrow Gauge friends," he whistled. Suddenly, a small green engine darted out of a tunnel.

"Hello!" peeped Thomas.

But the little green engine rolled away into another tunnel.

Thomas asked Skarloey about the green engine.
"His name is Luke. He hides here because he
did something very bad."
Thomas promised to keep the secret locked
in his funnel.

"What did Luke do that was so bad?" Thomas
wondered aloud later that night. "Don't worry,
Luke. I'll find a way to help you."

But Thomas wasn't really alone. Someone
was listening.

The next morning as Thomas chuffed to work, Luke emerged from a tunnel.

"Hi, Thomas," Luke said. "I'm sorry I hid from you. Will you be my friend?"

"I'd like that," replied Thomas.

Thomas and Luke worked together at the boulder drop all day.

"Why do you keep hiding?" Thomas asked Luke.

They didn't notice that Paxton was back. He was listening to Luke's story.

"I first came to the Island of Sodor on a boat," said Luke. "When they were lifting me off it, I bumped into a little yellow engine . . . and sent him splashing into the sea!"

Paxton couldn't believe what he had heard! He raced off to tell Diesel.

Later, Thomas heard Paxton telling Diesel the story.

"The yellow engine was never seen again," said Diesel. "We have to tell Sir Topham Hatt and Mr. Percival."

Thomas was worried. He had to find out what happened to that little yellow engine. Thomas chuffed to the Steamworks to ask Victor if he knew anything.
"That was me!" said Victor.

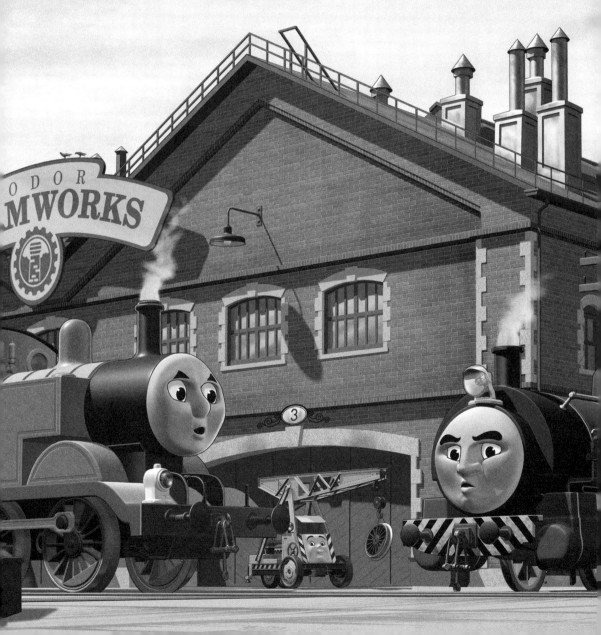

Victor's story about his trip to the Island of Sodor was the same as Luke's—except for one important detail.

"My chains were broken!" Victor said. "That's why I fell into the sea. But Cranky fished me out."

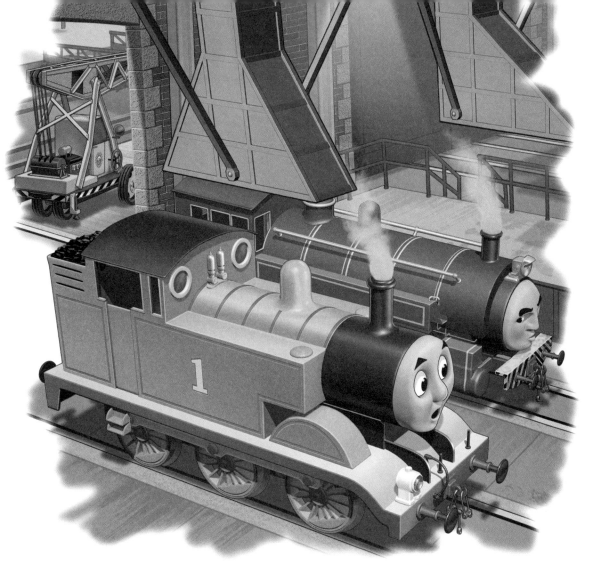

"So it was an accident!" peeped Thomas. "And you were repaired!"

"Yes," replied Victor. "I chose to be painted a new color—red!"

"I'm glad I found you," Thomas said. "Luke needs your help."

Diesel tracked down Luke at the quarry. Luke rolled up the narrow gauge tracks to get away. Diesel couldn't follow.

"You can't hide!" shouted Diesel. "Sir Topham Hatt is going to kick you off Sodor! Thomas can't save you now!"

"Yes, I can!" peeped Thomas.

The quarry walls were high, so Thomas needed Owen's help. Thomas was heavy, but Owen lifted him all the way to the top.

But Thomas' wheels were too big for the narrow gauge tracks! They skidded off the rails—and Thomas rolled toward a cliff! Just then, Luke came around a bend.

"Watch out, Thomas!" cried Diesel. "He's going to push you off! Just like he did to that yellow engine!"

"Don't worry, Thomas," said Luke. "I'll get you back to Owen."

Luke gently pulled Thomas back toward the platform.

"You're doing it!" peeped Thomas. Luke felt strong. He pulled Thomas to Owen, but the two engines weighed too much. The platform began to drop straight down!

Owen worked his hardest. Gears whined. Sparks flew. He stopped the platform before it hit the ground. Thomas and Luke were safe! All the engines cheered, except for Diesel.

Just then, Sir Topham Hatt and Mr. Percival arrived. They were confused and angry.

"Luke is a bad engine!" said Diesel. "He pushed a yellow engine into the sea."

Victor steamed into the quarry. Everyone was surprised.

"Luke, you didn't push me," Victor said. "It was an accident. I was repaired and painted red."

For the first time in a long, long time, Luke was truly happy.

Sir Topham Hatt was upset with Diesel. "You didn't find out the whole story," he said. "What really happened is what really matters."

"Well done, Thomas," said Sir Topham Hatt. "Today is a happy day for Mr. Percival and his engines." Thomas and all his friends, new and old, whistled happily.